W9-CBC-031

Phyllis Root • Pictures by **Margot Apple**

The Name Quilt

Farrar, Straus and Giroux • New York

For my Aunt Avonelle,
who remembers all the names on the name quilt
—P.R.

For Phyllis. At long last!
—M.A.

Text copyright © 2003 by Phyllis Root
Pictures copyright © 2003 by Margot Apple
All rights reserved
Distributed in Canada by Douglas & McIntyre Ltd.
Color separations by Phoenix Color Corporation
Printed and bound in the United States of America by Phoenix Color Corporation
Designed by Barbara Grzeslo
First edition, 2003
3 5 7 9 10 8 6 4 2

Library of Congress Cataloging-in-Publication Data
Root, Phyllis.
    The name quilt / Phyllis Root ; pictures by Margot Apple.
        p. cm.
    Summary: One of Sadie's favorite things to do when she visits her grandmother is to hear stories about the family
members whose names are on a special quilt that Grandma had made, so Sadie is very sad when the quilt is blown
away in a storm.
    ISBN 0-374-35484-7
    [1. Quilts—Fiction. 2. Grandmothers—Fiction.] I. Apple, Margot, ill. II. Title.

PZ7.R6784 Nam 2003
[E]—dc21
                                                                                                        2002069328

Summer evenings, after Sadie and Grandma chased
fireflies and drank lemonade and wished on the first
star, came the best part of vacations at Grandma's.

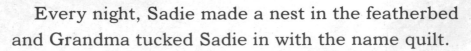

Every night, Sadie made a nest in the featherbed and Grandma tucked Sadie in with the name quilt.

The name quilt was made of little patches, like Grandma's other quilts. But the name quilt had names on it, too, sewn on some of the patches in tiny stitches with different-colored thread. And every name had a story.

Sadie would find a name on the quilt and trace the letters with her finger. "Francis," she would say. "Tell me about Francis."

"That was your grandpa's name," Grandma would say. "He died when you were just a little thing. When your momma was little, he used to take her to the woods to get walnuts. 'Want to go throw up?' he'd ask her. Then they'd go throw sticks up at the trees to make the walnuts fall. Did I tell you about the time there was a bear in the walnut tree?"

"Tell it again," Sadie said, and Grandma did.

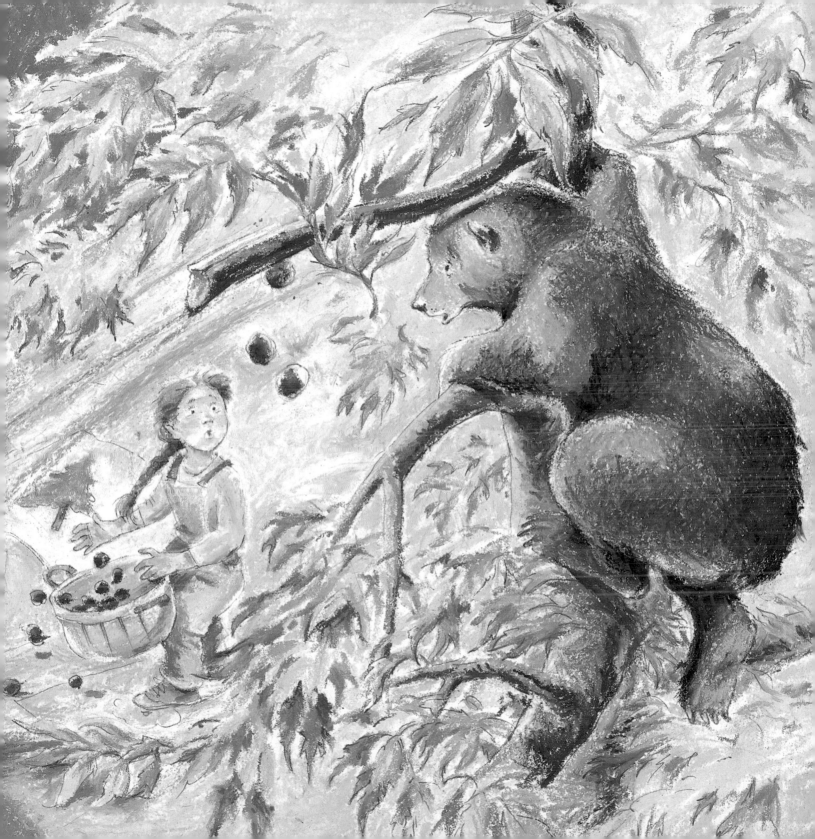

Sadie found another name, this one in fancy blue stitching.

"Tell me about Avonelle," Sadie said.

"That's your Aunt Nell, your momma's younger sister. She used to ride the hogs. This patch here with the little pink roses is from the dress she ripped one day when she fell off in the mud. You remind me a lot of Avonelle," Grandma said with a smile. "Good thing we don't have hogs anymore."

Grandma had a million stories in that quilt. There was a piece of the skirt Sadie's momma got blackberry juice on when she was a little girl and fed her piecrusts to Rosie the cat.

There was even a piece of Grandma's wedding dress, though it didn't look much different from all the other patches in the quilt.

"We didn't have money for fancy dresses back then," Grandma said. "My momma made my wedding dress, and my sister, that's your great-aunt Ida, picked the flowers for my bouquet from our own garden."

Even after Grandma kissed Sadie good night and left the room, Sadie could still trace the letters of the names in the dark. They felt like friends if she ever got lonesome listening to the crickets and the frogs and the owls.

Then a terrible thing happened.

It happened on a summer day so fine Sadie wanted to shout and turn cartwheels all at the same time.

"A fishing day for sure," Grandma said. "Best I've ever seen. First we've got to do a little work, though."

So Sadie helped Grandma feed the geese and gather the eggs. Then they heated up the water and filled the old tin tub for Grandma to do some washing in. When all the sheets were hung out to dry, Grandma brought out the blankets, too, even the name quilt, and hung them over the clothesline.

"They'll get a good airing," she said. "Smell nice and fresh when we turn in tonight."

Grandma packed up some sandwiches and lemonade while Sadie dug worms. Then Grandma put on her fishing dress and Sadie put on Grandpa's old hat, and they went down the hill to the fishing pond.

They fished all afternoon. The fish weren't biting much, so after a while Grandma lay back in the grass and closed her eyes, and Sadie did, too.

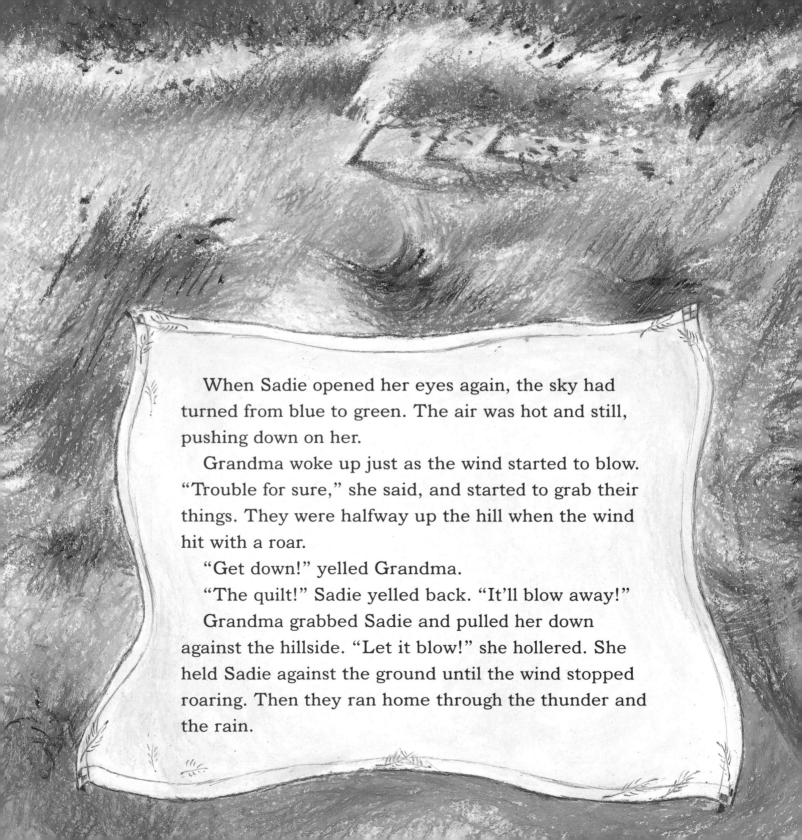

When Sadie opened her eyes again, the sky had turned from blue to green. The air was hot and still, pushing down on her.

Grandma woke up just as the wind started to blow. "Trouble for sure," she said, and started to grab their things. They were halfway up the hill when the wind hit with a roar.

"Get down!" yelled Grandma.

"The quilt!" Sadie yelled back. "It'll blow away!"

Grandma grabbed Sadie and pulled her down against the hillside. "Let it blow!" she hollered. She held Sadie against the ground until the wind stopped roaring. Then they ran home through the thunder and the rain.

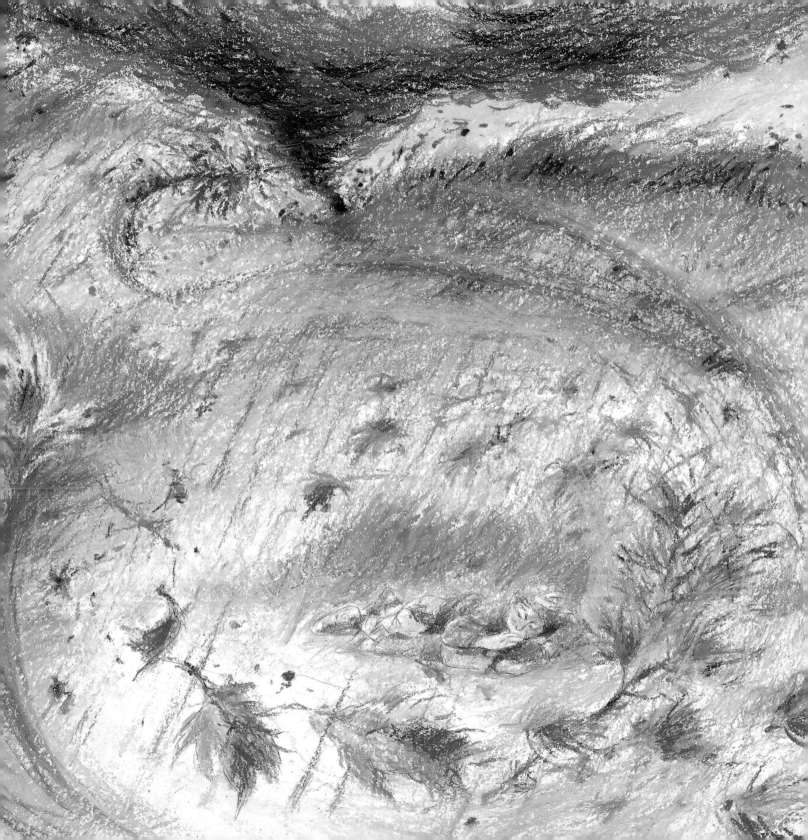

"Thank the Lord," Grandma said when she saw the house still in one piece.

But the whole clothesline, sheets, blankets, and name quilt, the beautiful name quilt, had all blown away. Nothing was left but the clothesline pole.

The wind had taken some shingles off Grandma's roof, too, and one of the geese was missing.

Grandma and Sadie spent the rest of the day picking up pieces of things that had scattered over the yard. Sadie looked all over the fields and in the woods for the name quilt, but she couldn't find so much as a scrap.

"It's all right," Grandma said. "We're still here. That's what matters."

Grandma made up the beds with old sheets, but her bed felt lonely to Sadie when Grandma tucked her in.

"So who do you want to hear about tonight?" Grandma asked.

"But, Grandma," Sadie said, "it's gone. The quilt, the names, the stories, all of it."

"Hush your crying now," Grandma said, patting Sadie's hand. "You think I need a quilt to remember for me? I keep all of those names and all of those stories right here inside of me."

"How?" Sadie asked.

"You just listen, you'll see," Grandma said. "So do you want a story tonight or not?"

Sadie closed her eyes and tried to see the quilt in her mind. Down in one corner on an orange-striped patch were the letters IDA.

"Tell me about Ida," Sadie said.

Grandma smiled. "Did I ever tell you about the time Ida ran over a hornet's nest? She just kept running and never got a sting. But Clayton, who was right behind her, he got so many stings he had to sit in a tub of baking soda for three days straight."

Sadie closed her eyes again and traced another name in her head.

"Joseph," she said. "Tell me about the time Uncle Joseph caught a catfish at the fishing pond and got so excited he fell right in the water."

They sat up nearly half the night, both of them remembering names from the quilt. Grandma had a story for every name, some Sadie had never heard before. Finally Grandma said, "Time to sleep. We've got to hammer some shingles on the roof tomorrow morning."

"You were right, Grandma," Sadie said. "You don't need a quilt to remember for you."

"Neither do you," Grandma said. "You've got all those names and stories inside of you, too. But a quilt is a good thing to have."

"We could make a new one," said Sadie.

The day after the terrible wind, Sadie got out
Grandma's scrap bag. Grandma got out the scissors,
a ruler, a spool of thread, and two needles. Together
they started on the new quilt.

It had a piece of Grandma's best fishing dress and a
piece of the shirt Sadie tore when they nailed the
shingles back on the roof.

Summer evenings, after Grandma and Sadie counted cricket calls and drank lemonade and wished on the first star, they worked on the quilt. By the end of the summer, they had stitched together all the scraps and sewed on all the names from the quilt the wind took.

They stitched a new name on the name quilt, too.
Right in the center, on a piece with yellow stars,
Grandma helped Sadie sew on her very own name.